D1645014

The Big Book of Friendship Stories

ORCHARD

ORCHARD BOOKS

First published in 2014 in Italy by Fivestore
First published in Great Britain in 2017 by The Watts Publishing Group

1 3 5 7 9 10 8 6 4 2

A CIP catalogue record for this book is available from the British Library.

HB ISBN 978 1 40834 478 1
PB ISBN 978 1 40835 364 6

Printed and bound in China

Orchard Books
An imprint of Hachette Children's Group
Part of The Watts Publishing Group Limited
Carmelite House
50 Victoria Embankment
London EC4Y 0DZ

An Hachette UK Company
www.hachette.co.uk

www.hachettechildrens.co.uk

Prologue

Twilight Sparkle, Rarity, Fluttershy, Applejack, Rainbow Dash, Pinkie Pie and Spike the dragon are the best of friends. Working together to maintain the peace and tranquility of Ponyville, their beloved home, they discover an important message – that true friends are always there when you need them!

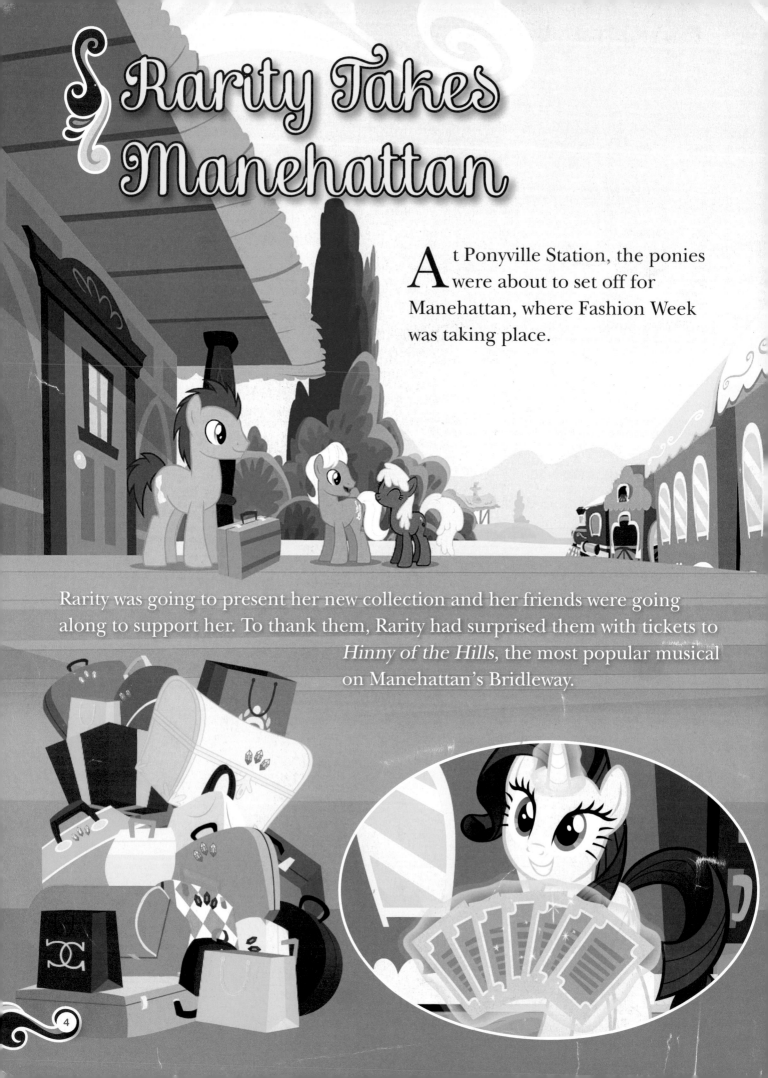

Rarity Takes Manehattan

A t Ponyville Station, the ponies were about to set off for Manehattan, where Fashion Week was taking place.

Rarity was going to present her new collection and her friends were going along to support her. To thank them, Rarity had surprised them with tickets to *Hinny of the Hills*, the most popular musical on Manehattan's Bridleway.

Once they arrived, the ponies left their bags at the hotel and went out sightseeing. As they strolled down the city's elegant shopping streets, Rarity imagined what it would feel like to have her clothes displayed in one of the gorgeous boutiques. "I would be the happiest pony in the world!" she said.

Rarity's friends asked if she needed any help preparing her collection, but Rarity was feeling confident already …

She had made a series of gorgeous outfits using a fabric that she had invented. All that remained was to present the collection at an interview with the judge, Prim Hemline.

Just then Pinkie Pie had realised that there were only ten minutes until the meeting. Now Rarity really did have something to worry about! "Oh no! I need to get all the way across town and if I'm late, I'll be disqualified! I need a taxi straight away!"

Unfortunately there was a sudden rain shower, so all the taxis were taken. But just as the ponies were about to give up, Rarity found a cab that took her to her destination in time.

Rarity ran on to the catwalk where Prim was instructing the competitors. "Go backstage and prepare your collections! Tomorrow there will be an elimination round and some of you will be sent home."

Backstage, Rarity was pleased to run into Suri Polomare, an old friend from the Ponyville Knitters League, who had moved to the city and become a famous designer.

Suri was impressed by Rarity's designs. "What an amazing fabric!" she exclaimed excitedly. "Would you mind if I took a sample? Just to add a few small details to my outfits."

"Of course," replied Rarity, who was always generous. "I'll give you a whole roll of it!"

Without a word of thanks, Suri snatched it and ran off.

Once Suri had gone, Rarity put the finishing touches to her own outfits. A few hours later, she joined the other competitors at the end of the catwalk. There she had a nasty shock: using the fabric that Rarity had given her, Suri had copied her whole collection and was now being praised by Judge Prim!

Furious, Rarity confronted Suri, who just laughed at her: "It was your fault for giving me the fabric. It's everypony for herself in the big city!"

Only Miss Pommel, Suri's assistant, looked sorry for Rarity – and was scolded by the treacherous Suri.

Rarity returned to the hotel in tears. But her friends comforted her and told her not to give up. They would help her to create some new designs. Eventually Rarity agreed. "We can use fabric and things we can find in the hotel!" she suggested.

With Rarity instructing them, the friends worked tirelessly – until Pinkie Pie pointed out that the musical was about to start. "Are you going to abandon me now?" howled Rarity. "Do you want my show to be a failure?"

Feeling guilty, the friends decided not to go to the musical. Instead they worked all night on Rarity's collection.

The next day, Rarity hurried to the Fashion Show – without thanking her friends. Her new designs were a huge success!

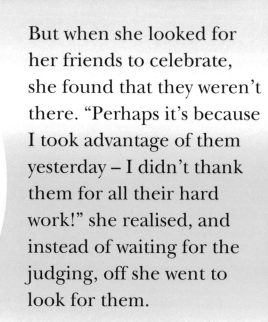

But when she looked for her friends to celebrate, she found that they weren't there. "Perhaps it's because I took advantage of them yesterday – I didn't thank them for all their hard work!" she realised, and instead of waiting for the judging, off she went to look for them.

Meanwhile the competition had ended. Just as Rarity reached the front door, Suri appeared, boasting about her victory. At the same time, Rarity's friends tumbled through the door. "We're sorry we're late! We fell asleep!" said Twilight Sparkle.

"What a shame you didn't win," added Pinkie Pie.

"Who cares about the competition!" cried Rarity. "I'm so happy you're here, despite me being mean and taking you all for granted."

But true friends always forgive, and the ponies hugged one another happily.

"To make up for my behaviour," announced Rarity, "I've organised an exclusive performance of the musical, just for you!"

So the ponies saw the musical after all – and at the end there was another surprise: Miss Pommel, Suri's assistant, came in and handed Rarity a trophy. "You were the winner all along!" she said with a smile. "Suri lied to you because she hoped that if you didn't claim the trophy, the judge would award the victory to her."

Miss Pommel felt guilty for helping Suri and asked Rarity to forgive her. She also had a present for her: a beautiful reel of rainbow thread!

Rarity knew she had learned a valuable lesson. Suri had behaved badly but Rarity forgave her anyway. She was proud of what she had achieved and, more than anything, she was happy that her friends had been there for her!

the end

Pinkie Apple Pie

In the Golden Oak Library, Twilight Sparkle and Spike the dragon were doing some research into the family histories of the inhabitants of Ponyville.

Just at that moment, Pinkie Pie appeared! She had been strolling nearby and had decided to pay her friends a surprise visit.

Pinkie Pie was curious about the piles of scrolls, so Spike the dragon explained.

"These are Ponyville's historical records: they explain where the ponies came from and how their families are related."

Pinkie Pie opened the ancient scrolls and began to read, and it wasn't long before she made an incredible discovery – she was related to Applejack!

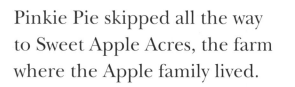

Pinkie Pie skipped all the way to Sweet Apple Acres, the farm where the Apple family lived.

Applejack was there and so too were her grandmother, Granny Smith, her little sister, Apple Bloom, and her big brother, Big McIntosh. Everypony listened as Pinkie Pie told them all her surprising news.

Applejack was delighted by the discovery. Pinkie Pie was one of her best friends and it would be amazing if they were related … but she thought it was odd that no one had known about it before.

Pinkie Pie produced a long scroll and Applejack read it carefully.
"It says here that my Auntie Applesauce was a distant cousin of the Pie family …
but there's a smudge on the page. I can't read exactly what it says – so we still
don't know for sure if we're related!" said Applejack with a frown.

"I do! I know I'm an Apple!" Pinkie Pie cried happily. The rest of the family shared her delight and gladly welcomed her into the family.

"I don't want to ruin the moment," interrupted Applejack. "But we need to be sure. How can we find out the truth?"

"I have an idea," said Granny Smith. "In her cabin, our cousin Goldie Delicious has lots of family heirlooms. She will definitely have the proof that we need!"

"Let's go!" cried Pinkie Pie. "It's time for a family road trip!"

As quick as a flash, the wagon was loaded up with baggage. But before they set off, Applejack warned her family: "Let's show Pinkie Pie our good side and not argue!"

Their good intentions didn't last for long. The Apples bickered continually! First of all, the wagon collapsed because Big McIntosh had overloaded it, and he got a telling-off from his sister, Applejack.

Pinkie Pie had the idea of building a raft from the broken wagon, so they continued their journey along the river. But it wasn't long before clumsy Apple Bloom dropped the map into the water, which had shown them exactly where to find Goldie Delicious's home.

Applejack scolded her sister then tried to take the helm. But it was Granny Smith who seized control! She narrowly avoided steering the raft into a cave full of monsters, and if that wasn't bad enough, then she sent them plummeting down a waterfall!

But Pinkie Pie took it all in her stride and carried on taking photographs for her album!

At last the five ponies reached Goldie's cabin. Their cousin wasn't at home, so they waited outside.

Pinkie Pie really hadn't seen the family at their best, worried Applejack. There had been so much arguing!

She hoped her friend wasn't upset …

Soon Goldie arrived and invited them inside.

It wasn't easy to get through the door: the house was filled to the rafters with family heirlooms and other treasures – not to mention all the cats that Goldie looked after!

Once they had made it into the living room, Applejack explained why they had come, and Goldie took out a dusty old book. While the ponies looked on eagerly, she found the page she was looking for ... only to discover that, like the scroll, it was damaged and almost impossible to read!

"So we'll never know for sure if I'm an Apple!" sobbed Pinkie Pie, disappointed.

"I don't care what the book says," Applejack declared. "After the adventure that we've had together, you will always be a true Apple!" The others agreed and they gave Pinkie Pie the biggest, warmest Apple-i-est hug.

A family photograph was the perfect way to celebrate! It looked fantastic on the last page of Pinkie Pie's photo album.

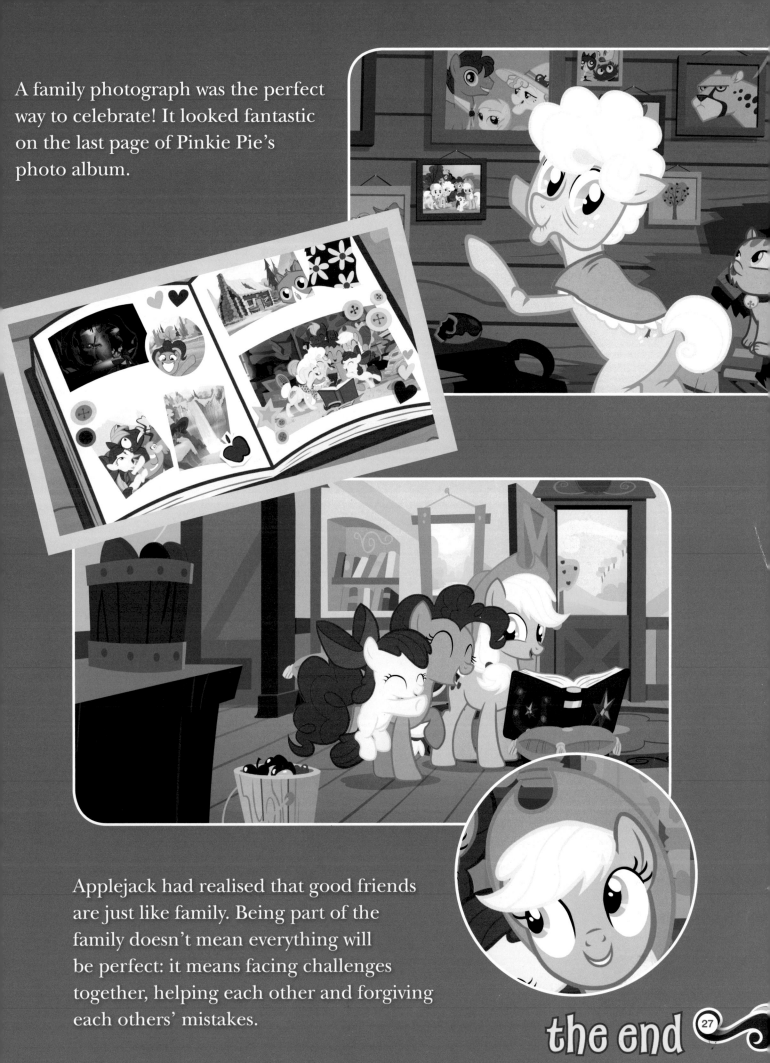

Applejack had realised that good friends are just like family. Being part of the family doesn't mean everything will be perfect: it means facing challenges together, helping each other and forgiving each others' mistakes.

the end

Equestria Games

It was almost time for the famous Equestria Games and the whole kingdom wanted to be part of the fun. Ponyville was going to be represented by Rainbow Dash, Fluttershy and Bulk Biceps, who were competing in the Aerial Relay.

The other ponies were very excited too. Pinkie Pie dressed up as a cheerleader to sing and dance them to victory. Rarity had made special outfits for them and Applejack had cooked them a batch of delicious apple pies.

Rainbow Dash was the most experienced competitor, so Bulk and Fluttershy listened carefully to her advice. But their first practice sessions were not a success – they needed a lot more training and they had run out of time! Today they needed to get the train to Rainbow Falls, where the qualifying rounds were taking place.

When they reached the stunning Rainbow Falls, they found the other competitors already training hard. They included Spitfire, Fleetfoot and Soarin, better known as the Wonderbolts, the flight acrobatics team who were competing for Cloudsdale. Rainbow Dash was on cloud nine! The Wonderbolts were her heroes!

Rainbow Dash and her teammates watched in awe as the Wonderbolts practised their stunts. "They're the favourites to win the Aerial Relay," she declared. "But if we do our best, we could be winners too!"

The Ponyville team got back to work – but it wasn't going well. Fluttershy and Bulk kept dropping the horseshoe that they were supposed to pass to each other and carry to the finishing line.

"Watch out or we'll be disqualified!" warned Rainbow Dash anxiously. "Let's watch the Wonderbolts and try to learn something."

Up above them, Soarin was practising some daring moves when, all of a sudden, he lost his concentration and hit an obstacle. He was plummeting through the sky to the ground when Rainbow Dash swooped bravely to his rescue.

All was well that ended well, but Soarin had hurt his wing badly.

"I won't be able to fly for a while, but I'm sure it'll be better by the time of the competition," he said, wincing with pain.

Spitfire and Fleetfoot were less optimistic. While Soarin was taken off to hospital, they asked Rainbow Dash to train with their team. Rainbow was flattered but worried that, with two lots of training to do, she wouldn't be able to give her best performance for Ponyville. But the Wonderbolts would not take no for an answer and Rainbow Dash reluctantly agreed to help them.

In the days that followed, Rainbow Dash trained in secret with both teams. They could not have been more different. Flying with the Wonderbolts was lots of fun and she recorded her fastest times. Fluttershy and Bulk Biceps couldn't get even the simplest moves right!

Rainbow Dash was tired and discouraged when Twilight Sparkle found her after training. Twilight had discovered her secret double life! "Your friends are counting on you, Rainbow. They need your support," she warned.

But just then, Spitfire interrupted. He had an offer for Rainbow Dash: "Soarin still can't fly, but if you compete with us, we will win the relay for sure!"

Rainbow Dash didn't know what to do, so she turned to Twilight Sparkle. "I can't help you," her friend responded. "Only you can decide."

The next day, everyone was surprised to see Rainbow Dash arrive with her wings and legs in bandages. "I had an accident and now I can't fly!" she explained.

Rainbow was taken to hospital and her friends came to visit straight away. "We're so sorry for you! Get well soon!" said her teammate Fluttershy kindly. "We've found someone to stand in for you and if we win we'll give you the medal, because we know how much it means to you."

When her friends had left, Rainbow Dash made a surprising discovery. In the bed next to hers was Soarin ... and even more surprising ... he was completely recovered! It seemed that Spitfire had lied. But why?

"He didn't think I would be able to fly as fast as usual," Soarin told her. "You are very lucky to have such true friends, who want only the best for you."

Rainbow Dash understood that she had made a big mistake ...

... and tore off her bandages!

"I'm so sorry!" she cried, catching up with her friends. "I pretended to be injured so that I didn't have to choose between two teams! But now I know I want to be with you!"

It only remained for Soarin to be reunited with Spitfire and the Wonderbolts, and now that the teams were complete, the competition could finally begin.

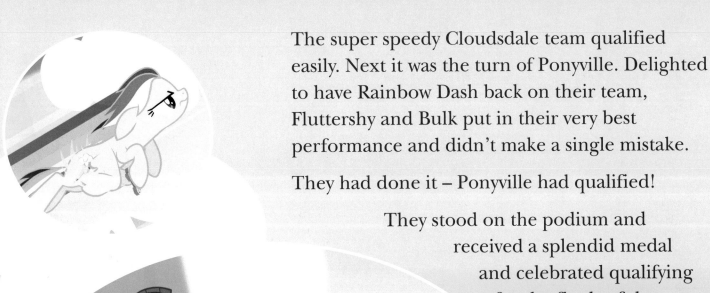

The super speedy Cloudsdale team qualified easily. Next it was the turn of Ponyville. Delighted to have Rainbow Dash back on their team, Fluttershy and Bulk put in their very best performance and didn't make a single mistake.

They had done it – Ponyville had qualified!

They stood on the podium and received a splendid medal and celebrated qualifying for the finals of the Equestria Games.

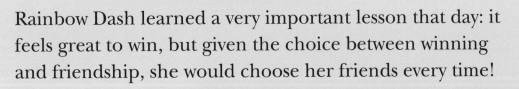

Rainbow Dash learned a very important lesson that day: it feels great to win, but given the choice between winning and friendship, she would choose her friends every time!

the end

Stage Fright

It was a beautiful morning and, as usual, Fluttershy was out in the wood, feeding the animals. The crisp air and sunlight brought a sweet tune to her lips and, once she had finished singing, all the little animals gave her a round of applause.

She thanked them with a smile – and then discovered that her friends had been listening too! They were standing with their mouths open wide, for none of them had heard such a beautiful voice before.

Once she had recovered from her surprise, Rarity suggested that Fluttershy should audition for the Ponytones, a singing quartet that would be performing the following night to raise money for the Ponyville Pet Centre.

Pinkie Pie agreed that it was a brilliant idea and urged Fluttershy to try, but the shy pony refused firmly.

Fluttershy explained that she suffered from stage fright. "I'm too scared to perform in public," she told her friends. "Remember how frightened I was when I first met you!"

Rarity was very disappointed that Fluttershy's talent would go to waste, but because she was a good friend, she didn't argue, and the ponies returned to Ponyville together to prepare for the fundraiser.

While the other ponies helped put up the decorations, Rarity and the other members of the Ponytones stood onstage and rehearsed their songs for the concert. They were so tuneful: it was going to be an amazing concert!

When they finished, Rarity told the other performers to rest their voices until their final rehearsal the following morning.

But when they met the next day, they discovered that Big McIntosh had lost his voice – he couldn't make a sound! Instead of resting his voice, he had taken part in the Turkey Call Competition with Pinkie Pie, who had won!

"You are the only one who can sing bass!" wailed Rarity. "We'll have to cancel the concert!" Without the Ponytones, the fundraiser would be a failure.

Fluttershy had an idea: they could ask the sorceress Zecora to help them. So they went to see her at her house in the Everfree Forest. Zecora told them that she could cure Big McIntosh – but it would take several days for his voice to return to normal.

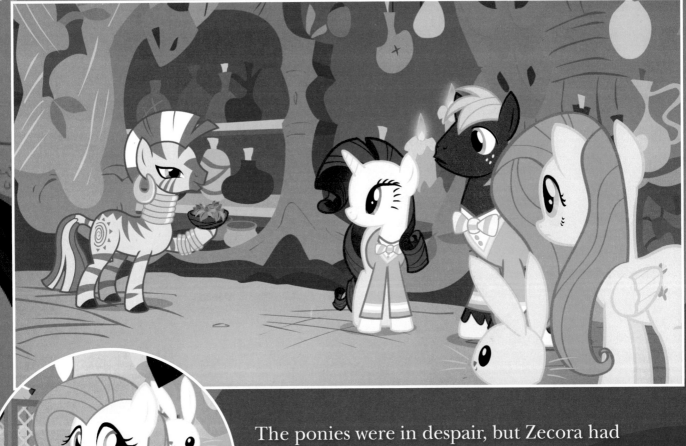

The ponies were in despair, but Zecora had another solution. If Fluttershy were to drink a potion made from the poison joke plant, her voice would become as deep as Big McIntosh's and she would be able to sing in his place.

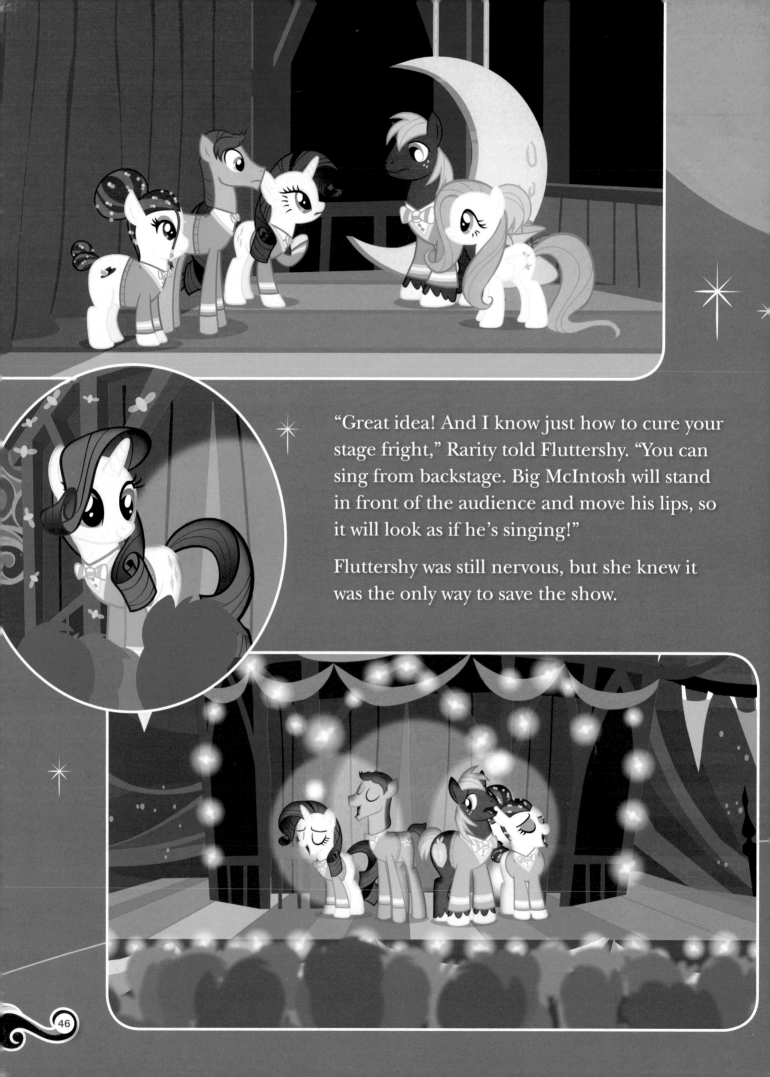

"Great idea! And I know just how to cure your stage fright," Rarity told Fluttershy. "You can sing from backstage. Big McIntosh will stand in front of the audience and move his lips, so it will look as if he's singing!"

Fluttershy was still nervous, but she knew it was the only way to save the show.

That evening, the main square was packed and the concert began
as planned. No one noticed that Big McIntosh wasn't really singing
and Fluttershy performed without any stage fright. The applause was
thunderous! The performance was such a success that the father of a young
pony called Zipporwhill asked the Ponytones to sing at his daughter's
birthday party the next day.

Rarity was about to refuse – she didn't want to put her
friend in an awkward position. But Fluttershy urged her to
agree, as she didn't want to disappoint the birthday girl.

The party was a great success and the Ponytones found themselves very sought after! They performed at Mayor Mare's ribbon-cutting ceremony. They gave a concert at Ponyville spa and another at Ponyville school. Fluttershy continued to perform in secret, concealing herself in ever stranger hiding places, and no one suspected anything.

A few days later, Big McIntosh's voice returned and Rarity thanked Fluttershy for her help. "You can take the antidote for the potion now and get your normal voice back," she said. But Fluttershy had been having so much fun that she asked if she could sing one last time, at a concert being held at Sugarcube Corner.

The Ponytones agreed, but that night Fluttershy sung with such gusto that she knocked down the curtain that was hiding her. The audience were astonished to see who the real singer was!

Fluttershy ran straight home and bathed in the antidote, which returned her voice to normal. But she was still horrified at having been discovered and told her friends that she would never sing again.

Gently Rarity told her that, once the audience had seen her, they had clapped her performance wildly. "You love singing," she said to Fluttershy. "Why give it up?"

Fluttershy decided to give singing a go and in the next few days she started singing with the Ponytones again – but only in front of her friends and the animals of Everfree Forest.

"Some day I'll manage to sing in front of everyone," she said, "but there's no rush. For the moment, I'm happy I've achieved this goal!"

Fluttershy had learned that friends help you overcome your fears. Slowly but surely, everypony will achieve their true potential!

the end

Creative Magic

All of Ponyville was busy preparing for the Foal and Filly Festival. Rarity had planned a special surprise to add to the festivities: a stunning puppet theatre that she had built with Spike's help.

But the reaction of Claude, the puppetmaster, was not quite what Rarity had been expecting. "I can't use this!" he complained. "The wheels are fake so I can't move it about, and the window is too small for my puppets." Rarity had made a theatre that was beautiful but not at all practical!

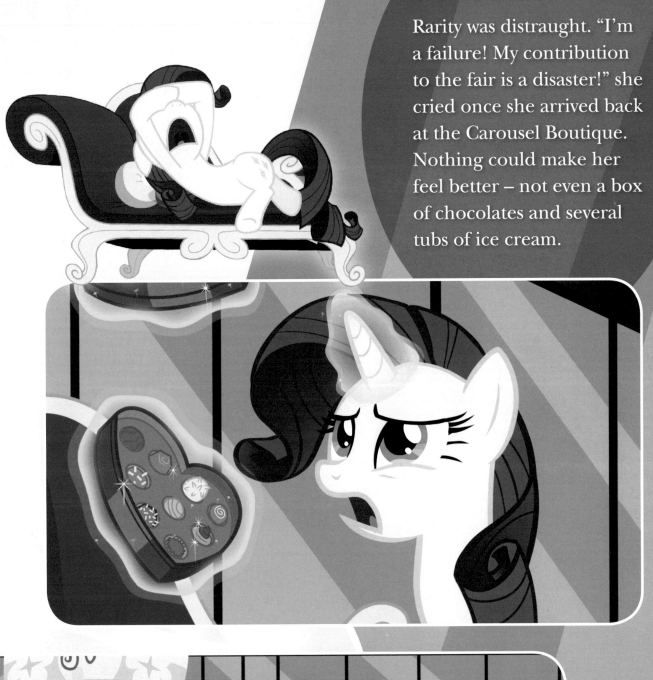

Rarity was distraught. "I'm a failure! My contribution to the fair is a disaster!" she cried once she arrived back at the Carousel Boutique. Nothing could make her feel better – not even a box of chocolates and several tubs of ice cream.

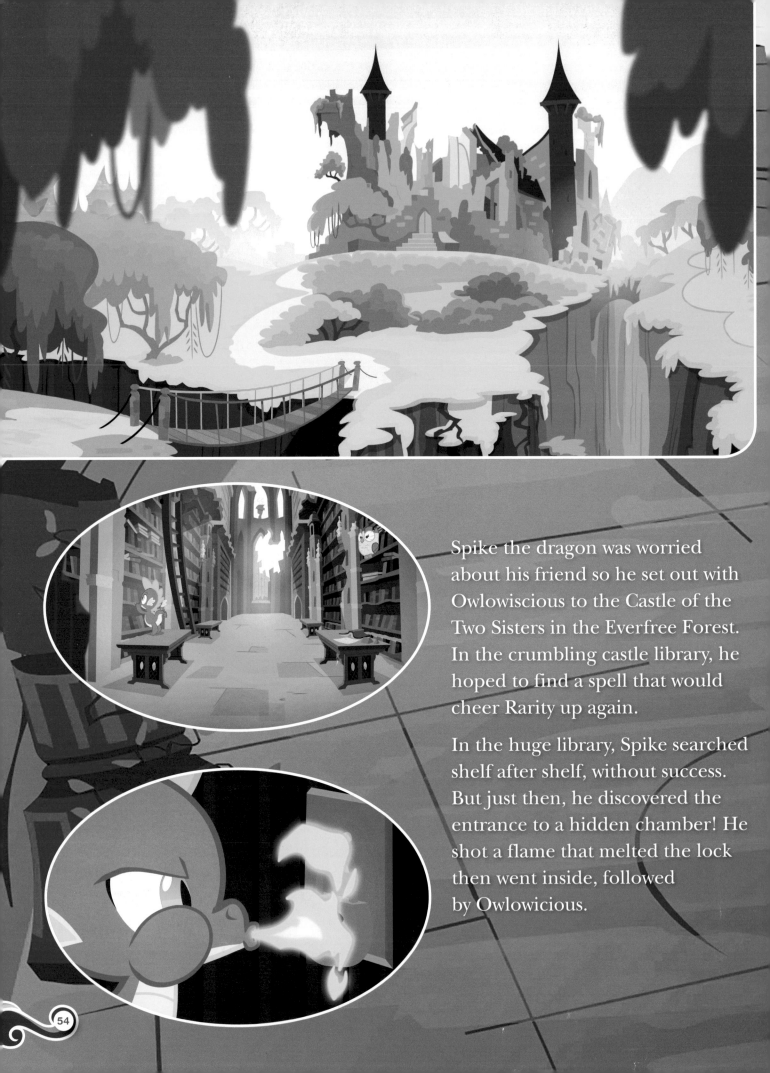

Spike the dragon was worried about his friend so he set out with Owlowiscious to the Castle of the Two Sisters in the Everfree Forest. In the crumbling castle library, he hoped to find a spell that would cheer Rarity up again.

In the huge library, Spike searched shelf after shelf, without success. But just then, he discovered the entrance to a hidden chamber! He shot a flame that melted the lock then went inside, followed by Owlowicious.

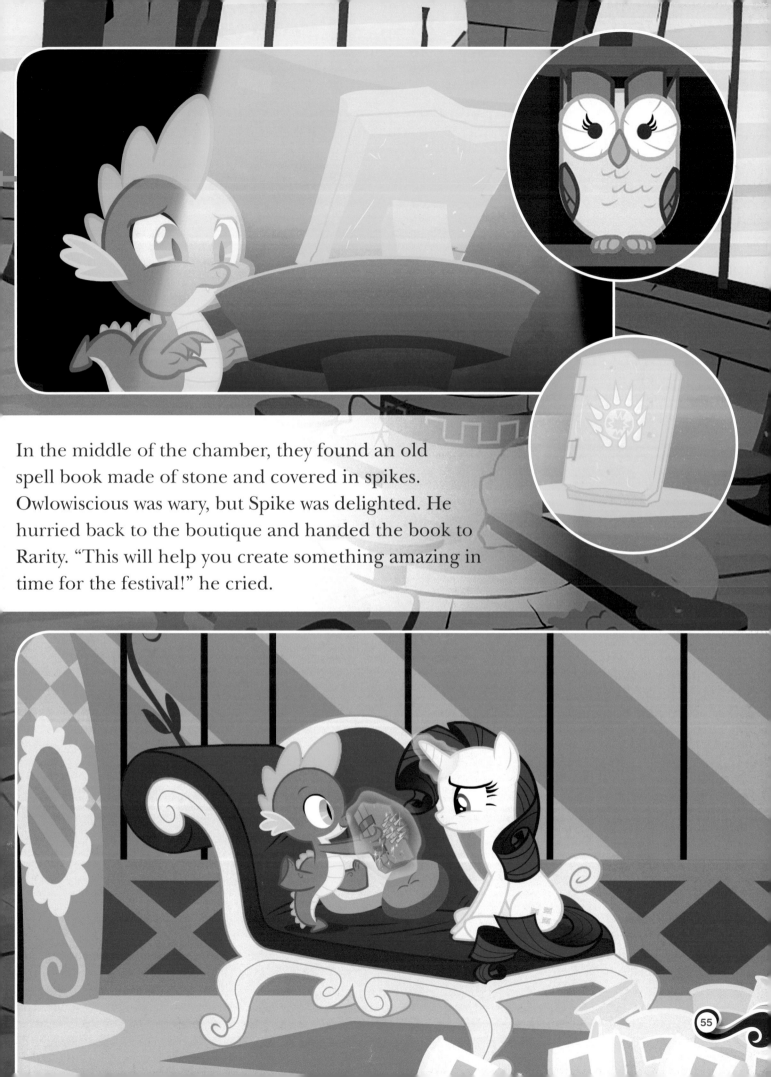

In the middle of the chamber, they found an old spell book made of stone and covered in spikes. Owlowiscious was wary, but Spike was delighted. He hurried back to the boutique and handed the book to Rarity. "This will help you create something amazing in time for the festival!" he cried.

No sooner than she had opened the book, Rarity found something extraordinary: a spell that would turn every thought into reality. It could only be stopped "when the truth is spoken". Rarity didn't understand this warning but she immediately felt a strange energy flow through her. She focused on the book … and, all of a sudden, its spikes became a beautiful cover!

"It works!" she exclaimed in delight. "Now I can fix the puppet theatre."

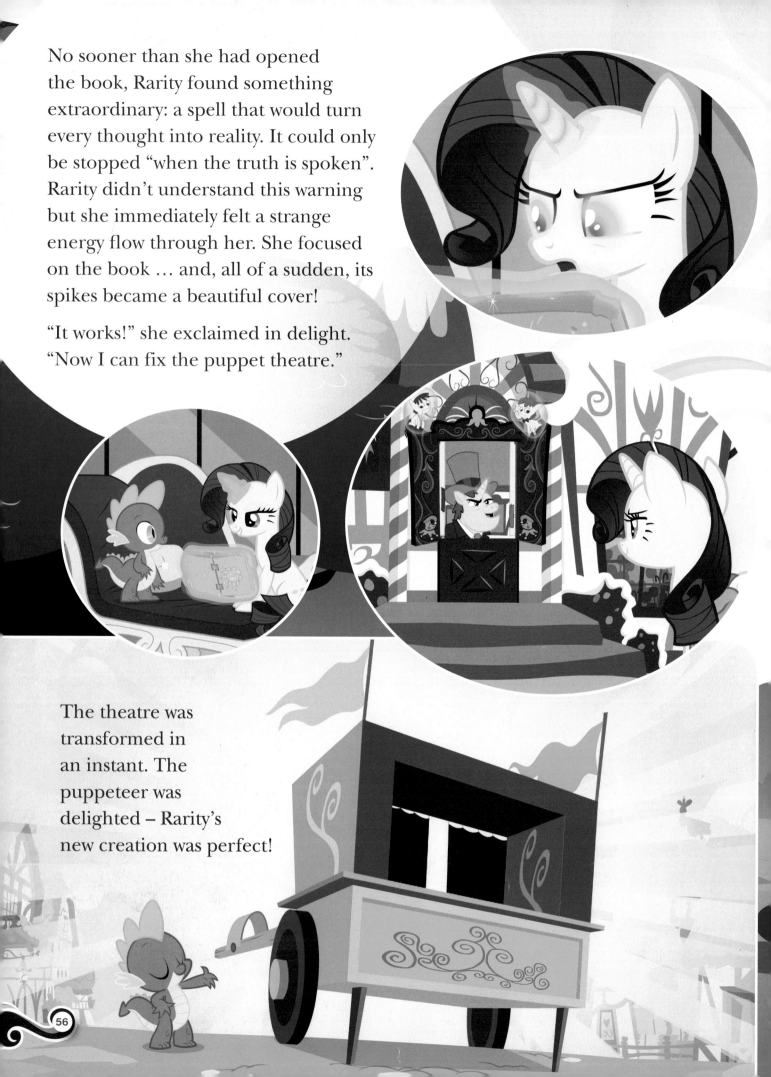

The theatre was transformed in an instant. The puppeteer was delighted – Rarity's new creation was perfect!

The festival went without a hitch and was a huge success. That evening Spike returned to the Carousel Boutique to fetch the spell book and take it back to the library in the castle. But Rarity asked him if she could keep it a bit longer and reluctantly, Spike agreed.

A few days later, Spike visited the boutique again. This time it was full of new fashion collections! Rarity had been creating outfits from noon till night – and now she had another idea: she would use the magic book to improve everything in Ponyville!

"Will you help me?" she asked Spike. "But you mustn't tell anyone that it's me making the changes, OK?"

Spike didn't want to upset Rarity so, nervously, he agreed.

Rarity set to work, transforming everything she came across: the Apples' comfy old cart became a heavy golden carriage. Fluttershy's welcoming little bird house became a bird mansion so big that the birds got lost inside it. The fun birthday bash that Pinkie Pie had organised for her foal friends turned into an elegant party, which the foals didn't enjoy at all.

Owlowiscious warned Spike that it was time to stop Rarity from using the magic.

"But I promised Rarity I wouldn't reveal her secret!" said the dragon. "I can't let her down!"

Things soon took a turn for the worse. Rarity paved the streets with gold, creating a fine powder that made everyone cough. Then she turned the town hall into crystal, trapping two ponies inside! Only Twilight Sparkle's magic could rescue them.

Rarity's creative magic was out of control! Spike knew he had to stop her, so when Rarity wasn't looking he seized the spell book. Rarity tried to snatch it back but it was too late – Spike had swallowed it whole!

But all of a sudden Rarity realised something: she didn't need the spell book because she knew the magic off by heart. "I'm going to make Equestria exactly the way I want it!" she cried ...

"... starting with you, Spike! I want you to be by my side all the time!" A strange green light shone in Rarity's eyes.

"That's enough!" cried Spike. "You've changed lots of things but you haven't improved any of them! I wanted to be a good friend so I didn't tell you ... but you've turned into a monster!"

At these words, Rarity's whole body shook – the magic was leaving her. At last she was herself again! "Thank you for telling the truth," she said. "That's what stopped the spell, just like the book said."

Rarity gave Spike the biggest hug. "Friends should never be afraid to be honest with each other," she said.

Spike knew she was right. We should always tell our friends the truth, especially when we think that they are making a mistake – a good friend will understand that it's because you care for them.

the end

Discover more spellbinding stories from My Little Pony!

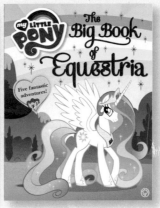

Orchard books are available from all good bookshops.
They can be ordered via our website: www.orchardbooks.co.uk,
or by telephone: 01235 827 702, or fax: 01235 827 703

ORCHARD

PRINCESS LUNA

Princess Celestia's younger sister, Princess Luna, rules the night. She is now discovering friendship after being banished to the moon for a thousand years.

PRINCESS CELESTIA

The ruler of Equestria lives in Canterlot Castle. She is as beautiful and kind as a fairytale queen, and she guides her beloved ponies wisely and well.

PRINCESS CADANCE

This sweet and kind princess has known Twilight Sparkle since she was a tiny pony. She is ruler of the Crystal Empire, and guardian of the magical Crystal Heart.

ZECORA

The wise and powerful sorceress lives in the heart of the Everfree Forest. She always speaks in rhyme and often has important advice to give the ponies.

DISCORD

The ponies' mischievous friend is a draconequus – a magical creature with the head of a pony and a body made up of lots of different animals.

CUTIE MARK

Everypony has a cutie mark that reflects their unique talent.

TWILIGHT SPARKLE

PINKIE PIE

RAINBOW DASH

APPLEJACK

RARITY

FLUTTERSHY